Let's see Ireland!

Sarah Bowie

THE O'BRIEN PRESS
DUBLIN

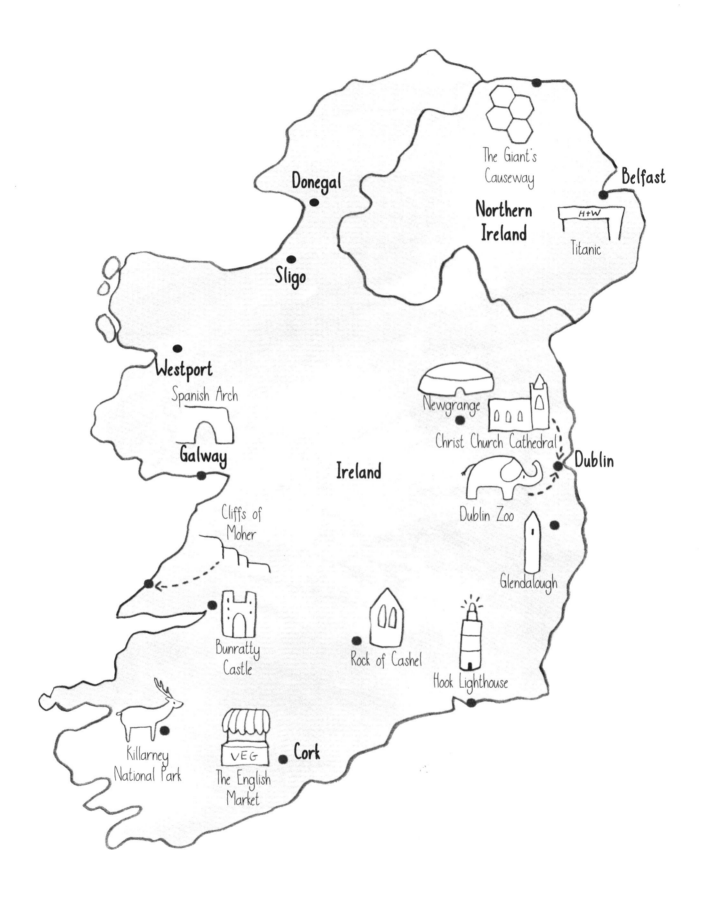

Donegal

The Giant's
Causeway

Belfast

Northern
Ireland

H+W

Titanic

Sligo

Westport

Spanish Arch

Newgrange

Galway

Ireland

Christ Church Cathedral

Dublin

Cliffs of
Moher

Dublin Zoo

Glendalough

Bunratty
Castle

Rock of Cashel

Hook Lighthouse

Killarney
National Park

VEG

The English
Market

Cork

Next up, Dublin Zoo, where hundreds and hundreds of animals live.

Glendalough – a long time ago
a monk called St Kevin,

who was friends with all the birds and animals, lived here.

That squirrel is having his lunch.

Hook Head Lighthouse

– it shines a light when it's dark,

so the ships don't crash.

The Rock of Cashel – Irish kings lived here for hundreds of years.
I pretended I was a king too.

Is somebody going to get an icecream?

These are the red deer who live in Kerry.
They are the BIGGEST wild animals in Ireland.

In Bunratty Castle you can see how
people lived long ago.

The Cliffs of Moher were the highest cliffs
I'd ever seen!

21

Spanish Arch in Galway is right beside the sea.

23

Stories say that giants built the Giant's Causeway so they could run across the sea to Scotland.

Belfast is where the *Titanic* (a giant ship that hit an iceberg and SANK!) was built.

Inside the passage at Newgrange we saw art from 5,000 years ago. It looked as good as new!

Home again.

And time to unpack.

Sarah Bowie is an illustrator, author and cartoonist who lives in Dublin. She is a founder member of The Comics Lab and her work has been published in a range of books, comics and magazines. She is also a big fan of pigeons and thinks they are smashing little creatures. Coo.

First published 2016 by The O'Brien Press Ltd,
12 Terenure Road East, Rathgar, Dublin 6, D06 HD27, Ireland
Tel: +353 1 4923333; Fax: +353 1 4922777
E-mail: books@obrien.ie
Website: www.obrien.ie

ISBN: 978-1-84717-731-5

6 5 4 3 2 1
20 19 18 17 16

Printed and bound in Poland by Białostockie Zakłady Graficzne S.A.
The paper in this book is produced using pulp from managed forests.

Molly Visited ...

Christ Church Cathedral, Dublin 2. You can visit Christ Church to see the tomb of the Norman knight, Strongbow – or the mummified cat and rat in the crypt that Molly saw.

Dublin Zoo, in the Phoenix Park in Dublin 8, is one of the oldest zoos in the world. The lion from the MGM logo was born there in 1919. Today it's home to over 400 animals.

Glendalough, Co. Wicklow. The monastery here at Glendalough 'Glen of the two lakes', was founded in the 7th century by St Kevin. Peep inside the Round Tower and churches, or go for a walk around the lakes – look out for the monster in the lower lake; legends say St Kevin chased him away, but you never know!

Hook Lighthouse, Co. Wexford is the oldest operational lighthouse in the world! It's also very close to Loftus Hall, Ireland's most haunted house!! Why not look out for fossils – the remains of little creatures from millions of years ago – like Molly found?

The Rock of Cashel, Co. Tipperary was the seat of the Kings of Munster for hundreds of years. You can still see the Celtic art and go into the medieval buildings. It's at the top of a hill, so you could see how fast you can run up to it!

There has been a market on the site of The English Market in Cork City since 1788. Today you can buy all kinds of things from meat, fish and vegetables, to crafts and clothes, cakes and chocolate – make sure to have something yummy.

You can see the Red Deer like Molly did in Killarney National Park, Co. Kerry (26,000 acres of mountains, forest and wildlife), but watch out for their antlers! And why not visit Killarney House and gardens or Muckross House while you're there?